# The Cow who Clucked

"I know nothing with any certainty, but
the sight of stars makes me dream."

—Vincent van Gogh

ISBN-13: 978-0-545-03539-2
ISBN-10: 0-545-03539-2

Copyright © 2006 by Denise Fleming.
All rights reserved. Published by Scholastic Inc., 557 Broadway, New York, NY 10012,
by arrangement with Henry Holt and Company, LLC. SCHOLASTIC and associated logos
are trademarks and/or registered trademarks of Scholastic Inc.

12 11 10 9 8 7 6 5 4 3                                        7 8 9 10 11 12/0

Printed in the U.S.A.                                        08

First Scholastic printing, October 2007

The illustrations were created using colored cotton fiber, hand-cut stencils, and squeeze bottles.
Book design by Denise Fleming and David Powers

# The Cow who Clucked

## Denise Fleming

SCHOLASTIC INC.
New York · Toronto · London · Auckland · Sydney
Mexico City · New Delhi · Hong Kong · Buenos Aires

One morning Cow woke up to find
she had lost her moo.

"The first thing I must do," said Cow,

"is find my moo!"

And off she went.

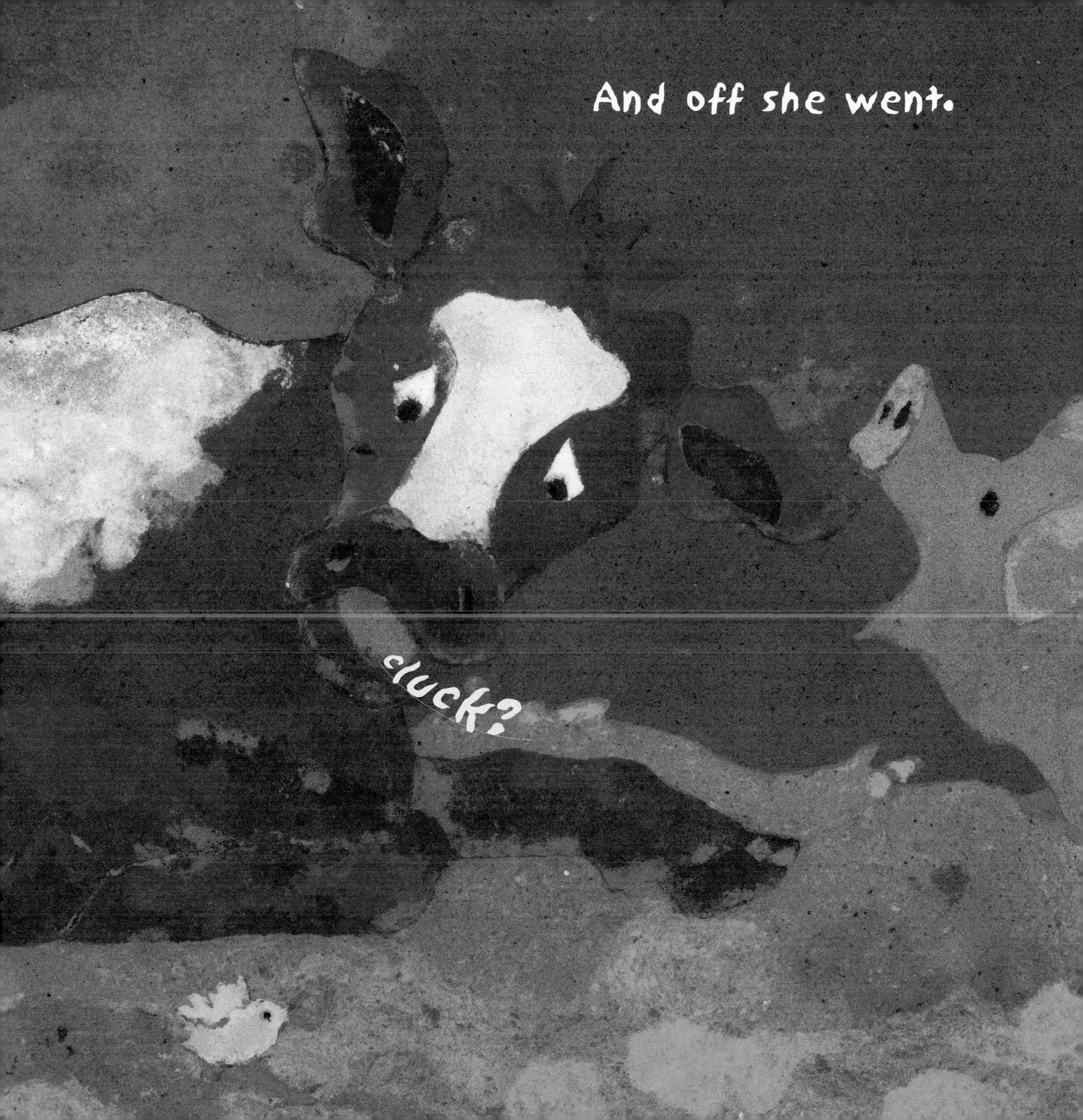

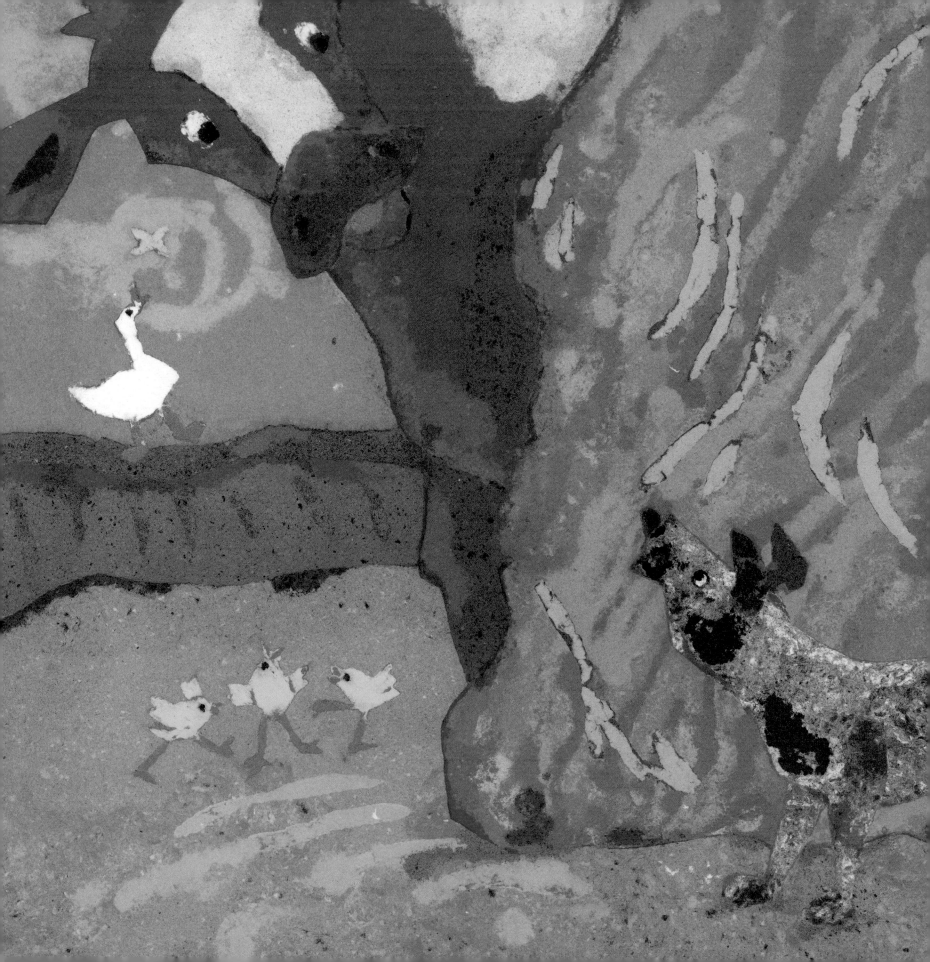

Cow met Dog.

"**Cluck, cluck,**" said Cow.

"**Warf, warf,**" said Dog.

"It is not you who has my moo," said Cow.

And on she went.

Cow stopped to nibble grass.
"Cluck, cluck," said Cow.
"Bzzzzz, bzzzzz," said Bee.
"It is not you who has my moo,"
said Cow.

And on she went.

Cow passed Cat.
"Cluck, cluck," said Cow.
"Meow," said Cat.
"It is not you
who has my moo,"
said Cow.

And on she went.

Cow cooled her feet
in the creek.
"**Cluck, cluck**,"
said Cow.
"**Glub, glub**,"
said Fish.
"It is not you
who has my moo,"
said Cow.

And on she went.

Cow spotted Duck.

"**Cluck, cluck**," said Cow.

"**Quack, quack**," said Duck.

"It is not you who has my moo," said Cow.

And on she went.

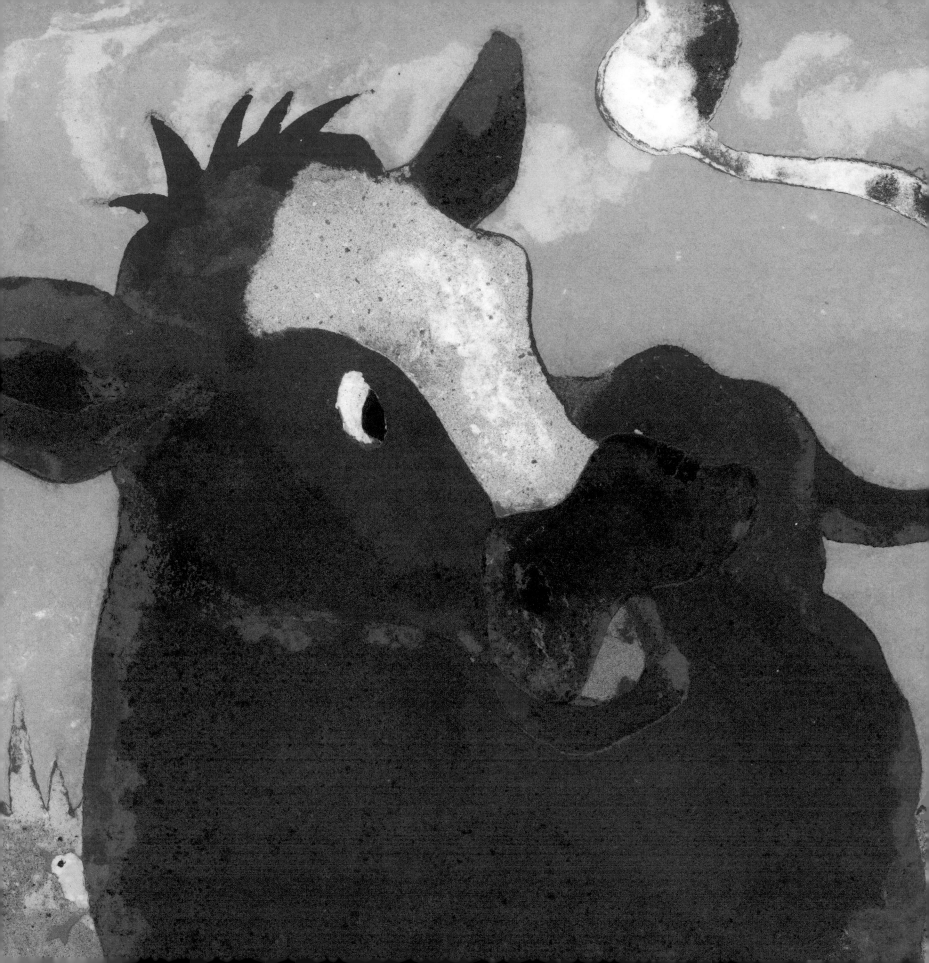

Cow crossed the meadow.
"**Cluck, cluck,**" said Cow.
"**Maa, Maa,**" said Goat.
"It is not you who has my moo," said Cow.

And on she went.

Mouse darted past Cow.

"**Cluck, cluck**," said Cow.

"**Squeak, squeak**," said Mouse.

"It is not you who has my moo," said Cow.

And on she went.

Cow stepped 'round Snake.
"Cluck, cluck," said Cow.
"Sssss, sssss," said Snake.
"It is not you who has my moo," said Cow.

And on she went.

Cow rested under a tree.
"Cluck, cluck," said Cow.
"Chee, chee," said Squirrel.
"It is not you who has my moo," said Cow.

And on she went.

Cow spied Owl.
"Cluck, cluck," said Cow.

"**Who, who,**" said Owl.

"It is not you who has my moo,"
sighed Cow.

And she headed for the barn.

Cow shuffled past Hen.
"Cluck, cluck," said Cow.
"Moo, moo," said Hen.

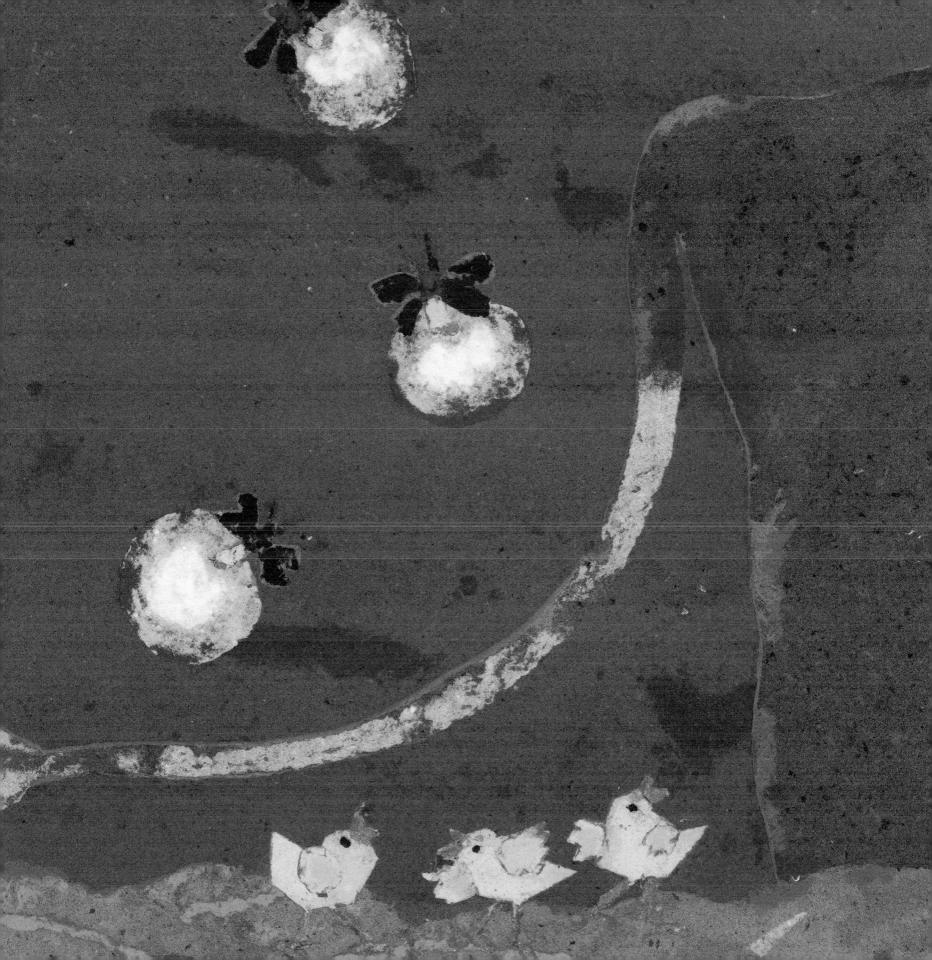

“Hen!” cried Cow.
“It is YOU who has my MOO!”

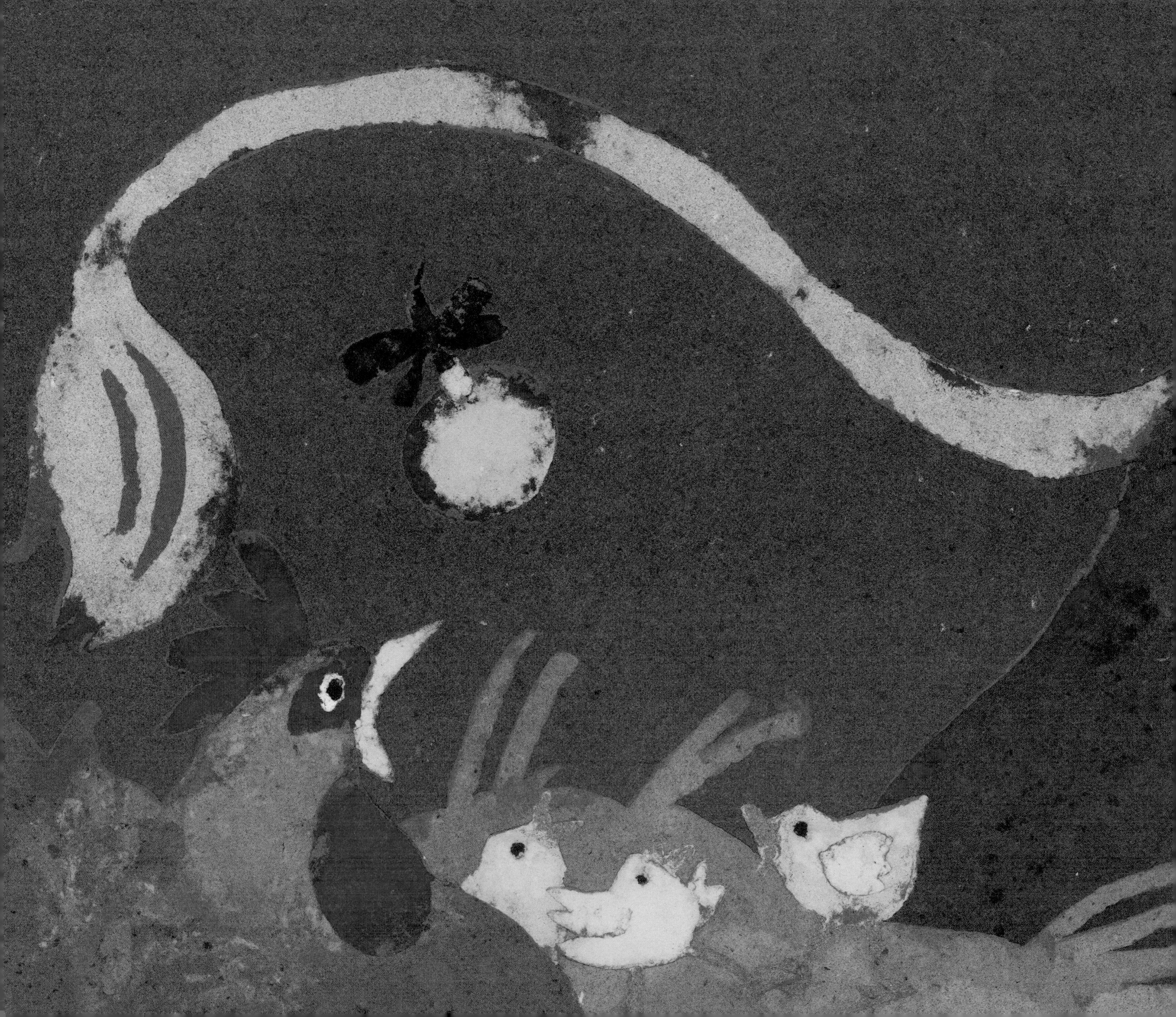

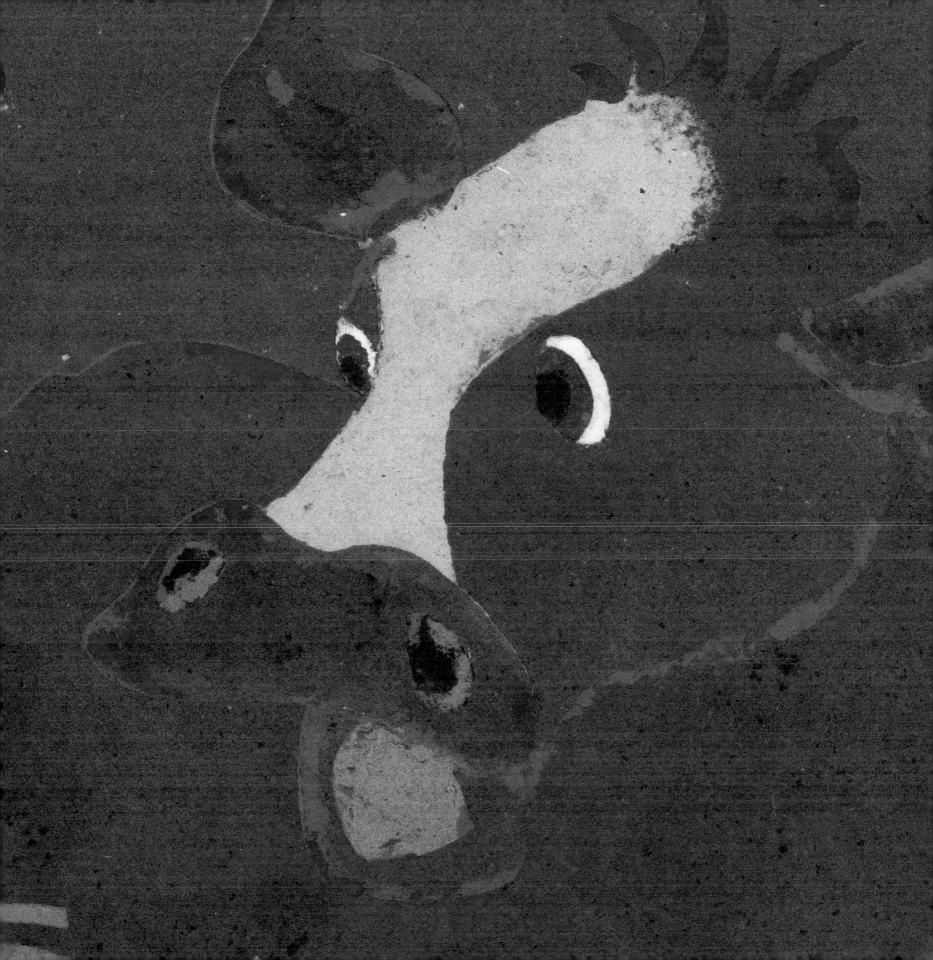

peep

peep

cluck